# imagine i

# having diabetes

Linda O'Neill

The Rourke Press, Inc.
Vero Beach, Florida 32964

NOTE: Not all of the children photographed in this book have diabetes, but volunteered to be
photographed to help raise public awareness.

Thanks to Jean Eichler of Stratham, New Hampshire for her assistance in interviewing.

PHOTO CREDITS
© Owen Mumford: cover, page 12; © East Coast Studios: pages 6, 20, 24, 26;
© PhotoDisc: page 11; © MiniMed: page 15; © Kingfish Studios: page 19;
© Eyewire: page 22

PRODUCED & DESIGNED by East Coast Studios
eastcoaststudios.com

EDITORIAL SERVICES
Pamela Schroeder

**Library of Congress Cataloging-in-Publication Data**

O'Neill, Linda
    Having diabetes / Linda O'Neill.
        p.  cm. — (Imagine...)
    Includes index.
    Summary: Discusses the causes and effects of diabetes and ways to control the disease.
    ISBN 1-57103-380-7
    1. Diabetes—Juvenile literature. [1. Diabetes. 2. Diseases.] I. Title. II. Imagine (Vero Beach, Fla.)

RC660.5 .O54 2000
616.4'62—dc21

                                                                00–025239

**Printed in the USA**

# Author's Note

This series of books is meant to enlighten and give children an awareness and sensitivity to those people who might not be just like them. We all have obstacles to overcome and challenges to meet. We need to think of the person first, not the disability. The children I interviewed for this series showed not one bit of self-pity. Their spirit and courage is admirable and inspirational.

*Linda O'Neill*

# Table of Contents

# Imagine This

You are always thirsty. You have to go to the bathroom all the time. You feel too tired to play with your friends. You are losing weight. These are all **symptoms** (SIMP tomz) of **diabetes** (DIE ah BEE tez).

*Being very thirsty all the time is a symptom of diabetes.*

People have known about diabetes for thousands of years. The cause of diabetes was not known until about 100 years ago. You don't catch diabetes. Type I diabetes is caused when your **pancreas** (PAN cree us) can't make **insulin** (IN suh lin). Diabetes is something that doesn't go away. You take medicine for diabetes and watch your diet.

*The pancreas sends insulin into your bloodstream.*

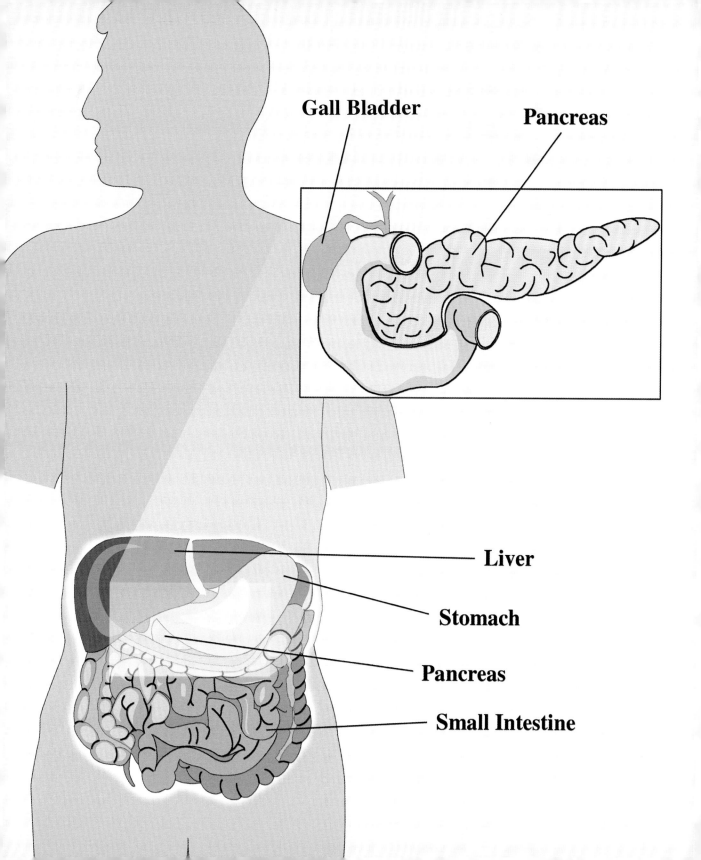

Gall Bladder

Pancreas

Liver

Stomach

Pancreas

Small Intestine

When you eat, your body changes food into **glucose** (GLOO kohs), a form of sugar. Glucose is the body's main fuel. Insulin's job is to help turn glucose into energy. With no insulin to do this job, glucose builds up in your bloodstream. This is called a high blood sugar level. When you have a high blood sugar level, your body, especially your brain, does not get the fuel it needs. You feel sleepy.

*You feel sleepy when your body doesn't have the fuel it needs.*

# Insulin

In 1922, Doctors Frederick Banting and Charles Best found they could use insulin from animals to help people with diabetes. Type I diabetes is insulin **dependent** (dee PEN dent). If you have diabetes, you must **inject** (in JEKT) insulin into your body every day. You can use needles or **syringes** (sir RINJ ez) that look like pens. With practice, you can make injections that don't hurt. Some people use an insulin pump. The pump is the size of a pager. It delivers insulin without using a needle. A tube is put into your body to deliver the insulin.

*Your body needs insulin every day. If you have diabetes, you must inject insulin.*

There are three types of insulin: short acting, medium, and long term. Sometimes, you take more than one type of insulin. You might take short acting insulin just before dinner. You might take medium acting insulin at bedtime.

*The insulin pump delivers insulin without a needle.*

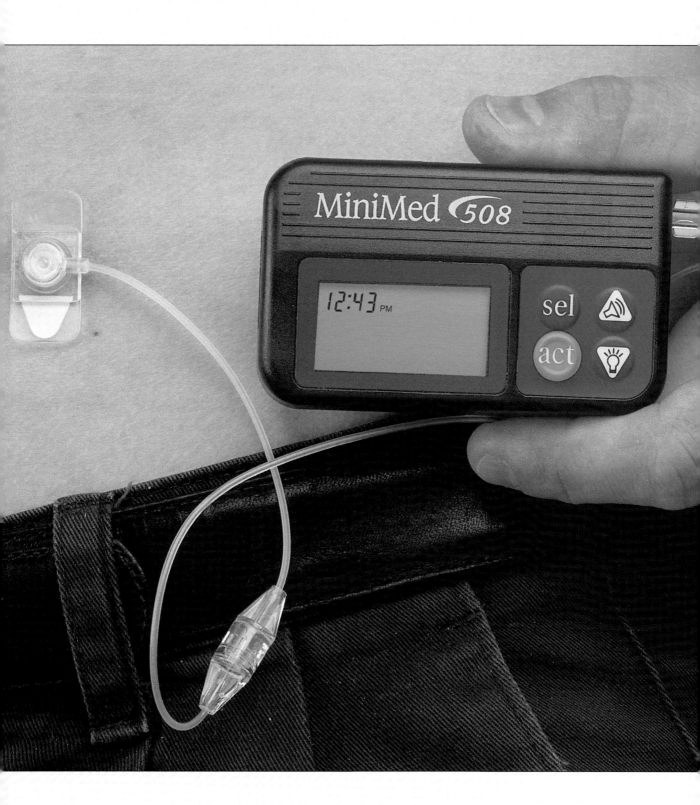

# Food Pyramid

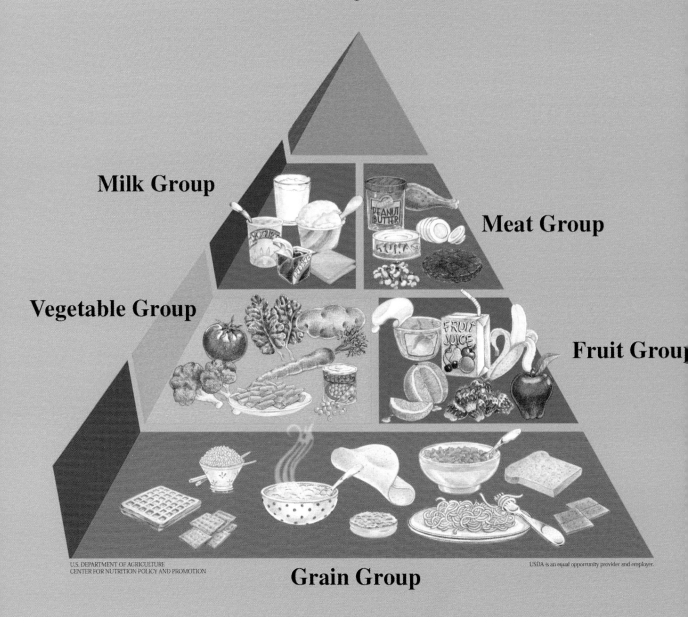

Milk Group

Meat Group

Vegetable Group

Fruit Group

Grain Group

U.S. DEPARTMENT OF AGRICULTURE
CENTER FOR NUTRITION POLICY AND PROMOTION

USDA is an equal opportunity provider and employer.

# Eating

Eating healthy is very important. Every boy and girl should eat meat, fruit, vegetables, milk, and starches like potatoes or bread. Three meals a day and a few snacks are just right if you have diabetes. It is a good idea to have snacks like crackers with peanut butter, pretzels or apples with you.

*A healthy diet is important for everyone.*

You can even plan meals so you can have a sweet treat like ice cream. You may eat a little less of something, or take extra insulin, or exercise more.

*Foods like these should be included in your diet.*

# Exercise

Eating raises your blood sugar level and exercise lowers it. Exercise is good for everyone. It helps make your body strong. When you ride your bike, your body uses glucose, like when you take insulin. Exercise can help you earn the treat you want. Eating a piece of chocolate cake will raise your blood sugar level. Jumping rope or other good exercise will lower it. If you are a young diabetic you need to exercise, eat healthy, and take insulin.

Type II diabetes happens in older people. They do not need to take insulin. However, they do need to eat right and get plenty of exercise. Their diet should be a healthy one with plenty of fruit and vegetables along with meat and milk.

*Exercise lowers your blood sugar level.*

# A Family Concern

Diabetes is a family **concern** (kun SERN). Your family needs to know what to do if your blood sugar is too high or too low. You place a drop of blood on a special paper to see what your level is. You must check your blood sugar four times a day. Very low blood sugar means you need something sweet. You can drink orange juice, eat a hard candy or glucose pills. High blood sugar means you need insulin.

*Eating sweets is part of being a kid. If you have diabetes, you need to plan ahead for sweets.*

If you have diabetes, you should wear a bracelet that says you are diabetic. It should have your name, telephone number, and your doctor's name. This will help in case of an **emergency** (ee MER jen see). The bracelet will tell nurses and doctors what they need to know to care for you.

You can be healthy and active by eating right, getting exercise, and being sure to take the right amount of insulin.

*Drinking orange juice helps when you have low blood sugar.*

# Meet Someone Special!

## Meet Alison

**Alison, how old were you when you found out you had diabetes?**
  "I was 6."

**How did you feel?**
  "I didn't understand what it was."

**Do you take insulin?**
  "Yes. I take it in the morning."

**Are you on any special diet?**
  "I'm on a low sugar diet."

**What do you do to keep healthy?**
  "I check my sugar level every day and try to get exercise."

*A medic alert bracelet will tell doctors and nurses you are diabetic.*

**Are there things you can't do because of diabetes?**

"I can't eat anything I want."

**Does diabetes make you feel different from other people?**

"A little, not a lot. At birthday parties, I can't have cake unless I take extra insulin."

**What would you like other kids to know about diabetes?**

"It isn't so bad, just a pain to have to think about."

## Meet Michael

**Michael, how old were you when you found out you had diabetes?**

"I was 5 years old."

**What symptoms did you have?**

"I had a lot of headaches and fevers. I was really thirsty. I went to the bathroom a lot."

**Do you take insulin?**

"Yes, I take insulin four times a day. Less if I'm playing baseball after school. More if I'm going to have pizza."

**What do you do to keep healthy?**

"I play sports. I check my blood sugar levels. I take my insulin when I'm supposed to. When I'm older, I'll lift weights. I don't know what else."

**Are there things you can't do because of diabetes?**

"The only thing I can't do is eat whatever I want. Everything else I can do."

**Does having diabetes make you feel different from other people?**

"Sometimes. Like, I have to eat even if I'm not hungry."

**What would you like other children to know about diabetes?**

"You get used to it."

# Glossary

**concern** (kun SERN) — something to pay attention to

**dependent** (dee PEN dent) — to need

**diabetes** (DIE ah BEE tez) — high glucose in the blood and urine
*Type I:* starts at a young age and needs insulin
*Type II:* starts at an older age and does not need insulin

**emergency** (ee MER jen see) — something that needs immediate attention

**glucose** (GLOO kohs) — a simple sugar used by the body for fuel

**inject** (in JEKT) — to put fluid into your body with a syringe, or needle

**insulin** (IN suh lin) — a hormone used in digestion, made in the pancreas

**pancreas** (PAN cree us) — a body organ needed for digestion

**symptom** (SIMP tom) — a sign, indicator

**syringes** (sir RINJ ez) — tubes with a plunger and needle to inject or take out fluids

# Further reading

Dalton, Cindy. *Why Should I.* Rourke Publishing, 2001

Patten, B. *Food for Good Health.* Rourke Publishing, 1997

Stewart, Gail B. *Diabetes.* Lucent Books, Inc. 1999

**Visit these Websites**
*www.childrenwithdiabetes.com*

*members.aol.com/CamelsRFun*

Owen Mumford USA
  *www.owenmumford.com*

MiniMed
  *www.minimed.com*

# Index